MW00952440

for John and Patricia

Annick Press gratefully acknowledges
the contributions of the Canada Council
and the Ontario Arts Council

Design by Karen Patkau

Canadian Cataloguing in Publication Data

Patkau, Karen
In the sea

(Annick toddler series)
ISBN 1-55037-067-7 (bound) ISBN 1-55037-066-9 (pbk.)

I. Title. II. Series.

PS8581.A8416 1989 jC813'.54 C89-094180-7
PZ7.P38In 1989

Distributed in Canada and the U.S.A. by:
Firefly Books Ltd.
250 Sparks Ave.
Willowdale, Ontario
M2H 2S4 Canada

Printed and bound in Canada by
D.W. Friesen & Sons

Printed on Acid Free Stock

In the Sea

Karen Patkau

Annick Press Ltd.

Crystal dangles sadly over the water.
Her glass figure blows
with the changing wind.
She longs to be in the sea.

Fish spring up from the deep.
They play in her colours,
and invite her to swim.

On clear nights the stars shine brightly.
Crystal gazes at them.
A bright light twinkles at her.
She feels so alone.

She drifts off to sleep and hears
a gentle star-song.
Music flows around her —
"Dive and soar with me."

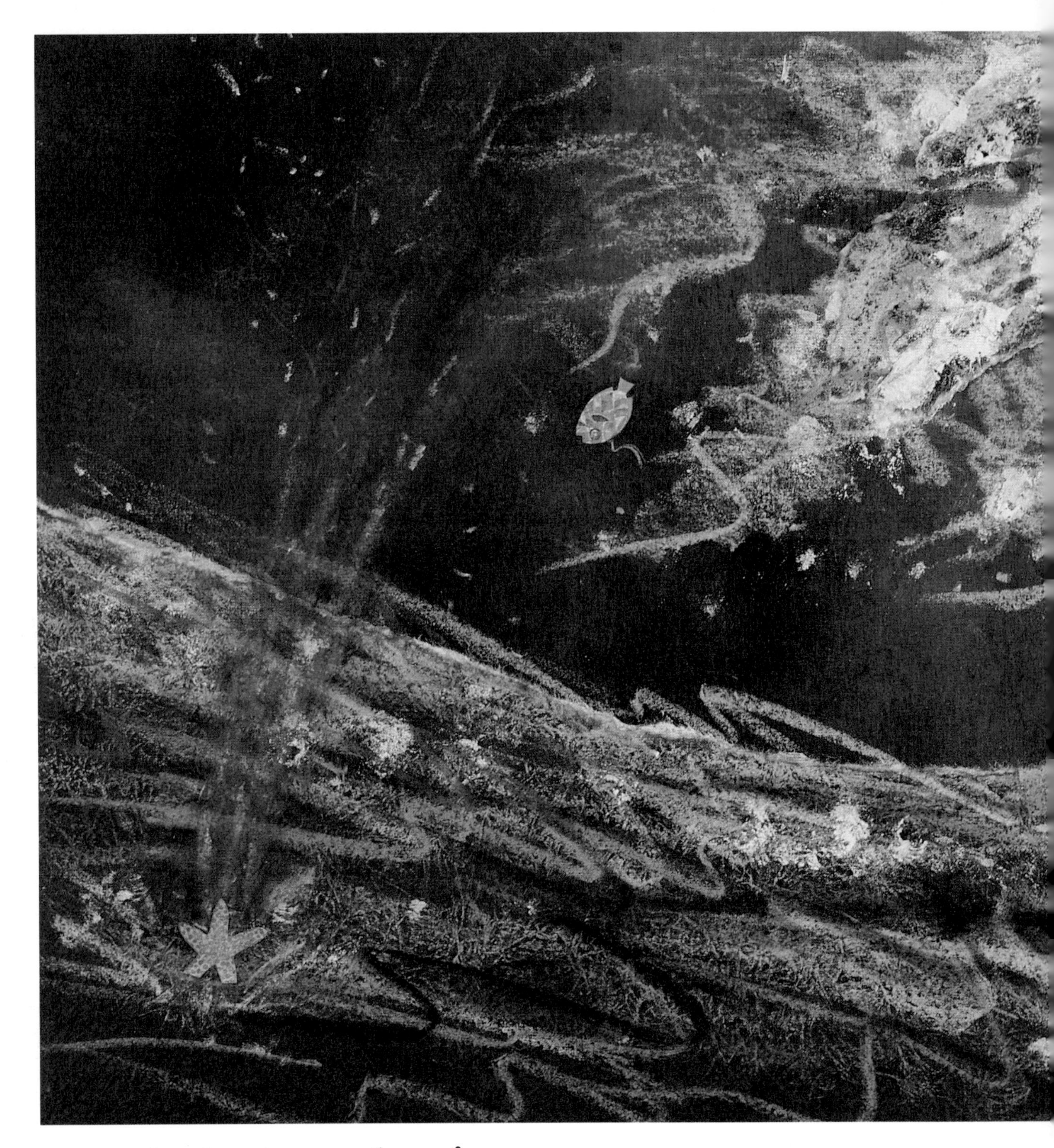

A dark storm begins.
Crystal watches with wonder
as her star falls into the sea.

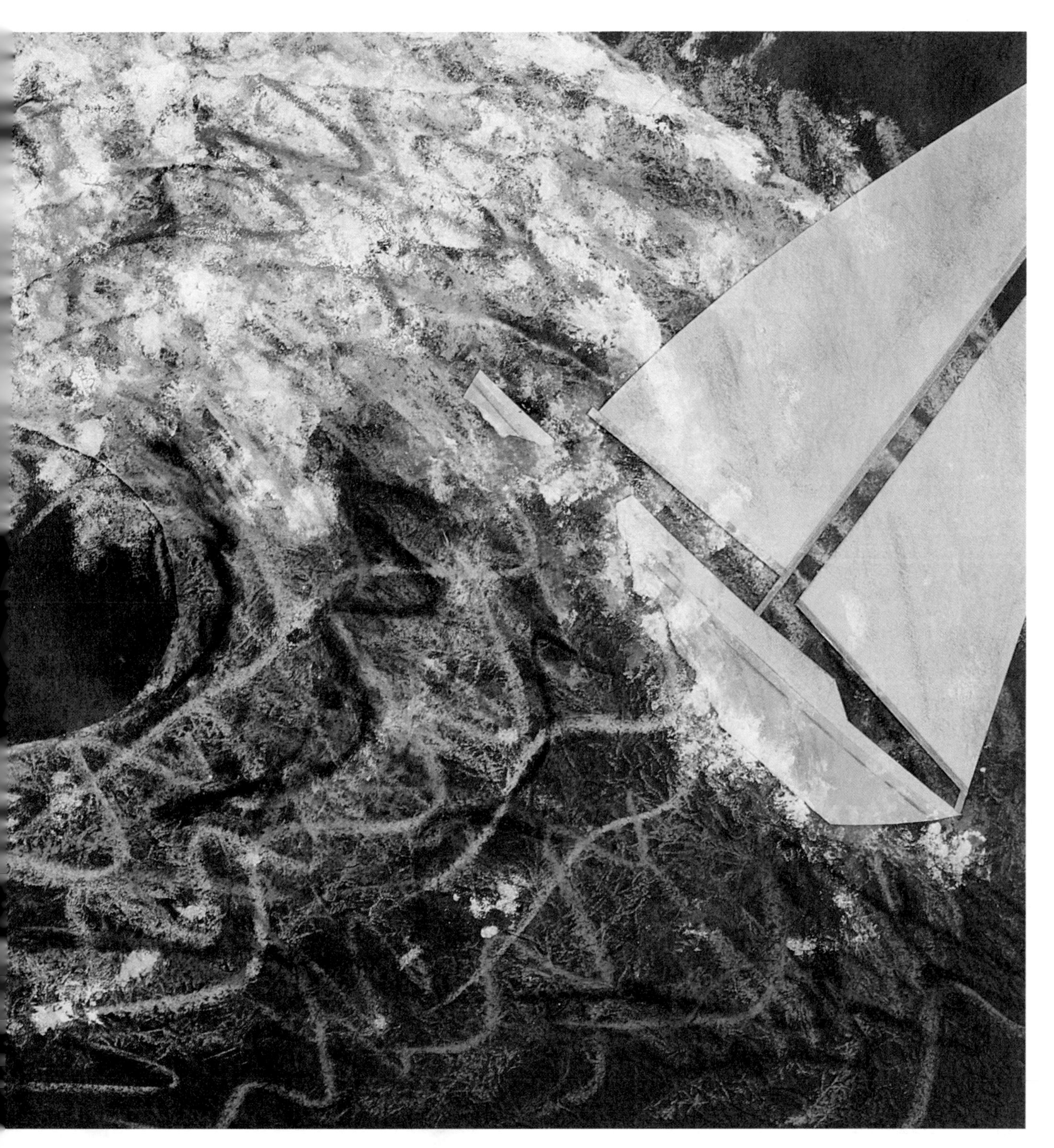

Crystal is tossed, toppled,
swept by waves.
She drops deeper and deeper still.

She lands with a thump on the bottom.
Lights sparkle, flash in the dark.
Crystal is frightened.

Soon the black water turns blue-green.
Creatures drift through a coral jungle.
A beautiful starfish is by her side.

Clown fish juggle and toss her about.
Crystal plays.
Starfish is always near.

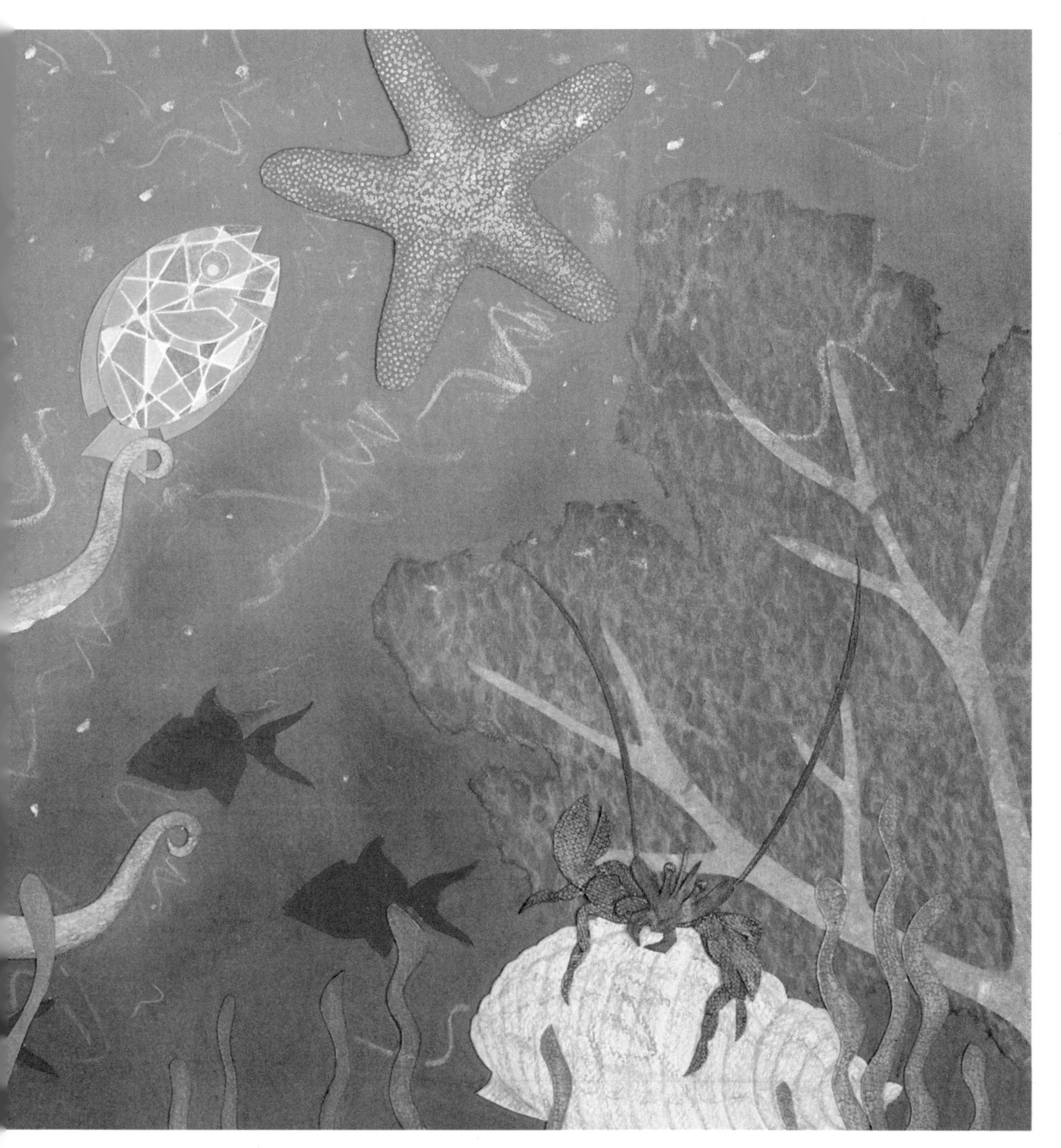

The friends explore this water world.
They dig tunnels and caves,
search for treasure.
They play tag with an octopus.

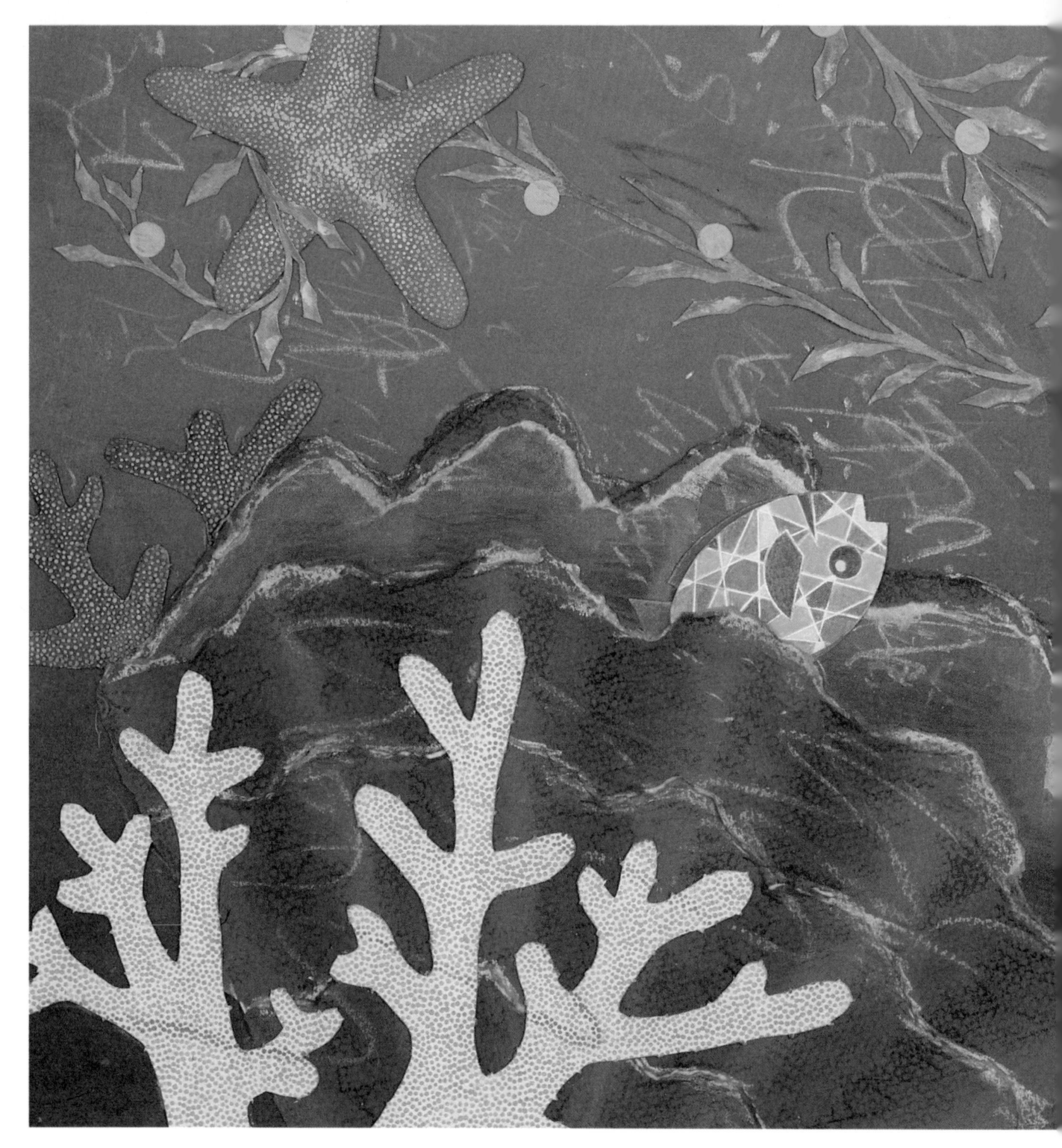

Seahorses take Crystal and Starfish
for a ride. Faster and faster they go.
Up, down, over and under.
Crystal loses her grip.

She spins and falls. Down and down,
into the jaws of a giant oyster.
The oyster snaps shut.
Crystal is trapped.

At night, when all is quiet, Starfish comes.
He dances on the giant oyster.
He sparkles and shines, tickles and teases.

The great jaws open. Crystal darts free!
She laughs, so happy,
and calls out to Starfish.
There is no answer.

Starfish is gone.
Everything is dark and still.
Her colour has faded.
Crystal drifts to the bottom.

A squid stops near her.
Crystal feels a flicker of light.
"Come," it whispers, "follow me."

Crystal follows upward, higher.
She begins to swim, up to the surface.
But as the sky darkens,
she thinks of Starfish.

She hears, once again, the star-song.
"Dive and soar with me."
Crystal looks into the night sky.

The stars are alive.
They make pictures in the dark.
Pictures of sea horses and turtles,
of porpoises and stingrays.

The bright star, the one she loves,
twinkles at her.
"Dive and soar with me."
And they remained friends forever.